CROSSROADS

Amira K. Wolf

AN ASCENDING INK BOOK

Cover art by Ricky Gunawan

Interior illustrations by
Jennifer Lange and Ameshin

Second printing, 2018

ISBN 978-0-9950487-2-0

www.amirakwolf.com
amira.k.wolf@gmail.com

ACKNOWLEDGEMENTS

First and foremost, I want to thank my mother for being one of the biggest influences in my life. Ever since I was little, she saw talents in me that I couldn't see for myself, or denied, up until not too long ago. She was always pushing me to go past my limits, but never shy to tell me the harsh truth and scold me when I had done something foolish. She is kind-hearted and nurturing, but tough and realistic; a unique combination for a unique person, which makes for an awesome mom.

I would also like to thank my aunt who has been behind me one hundred percent in any venture I undertook. She would read most of the things I wrote, give me feedback on what she thought, and corrected any mistakes she saw. I'm very grateful for everything she's done. Then there's my friend, Aaron Bos, who has pretty much become my unofficial editor. Like my aunt, he would review what I would write, but on a much deeper level. He would point out any and all flaws, but it was always with the intention of improving my writing and to lend me a helping hand. Therefore, it was never a bother to send him my work. It was a learning experience.

Next, a special thank you to J. S. for not only allowing me the use of his character, Locke Bellorne, but for also being the person who inspired me to write prose. At the time (and still to this day) my goal was to become a scriptwriter. Of course, I had written prose before, but it was either for school or as a casual hobby; nothing serious. However, it was because of J. S. that I added 'writing books' to my list of goals.

Finally, to my three siblings and those who have also supported me along the way (you know who you are), don't worry, I haven't forgotten about you. I just can't name everyone, it would be too long. Nevertheless, I still want to thank all of you, so… Thank you!

CROSSROADS

PART I

Locke firmly held onto the noblewoman's hand as they ran through the cavern tunnels. They had no more torches to light their way but, fortunately, the cave walls were lined from top to bottom with crystals that emitted a light blue glow.

Behind them, they could hear the quick skittering of several large creatures following them at an alarming rate. Locke knew they had to get out of there as fast as possible. He had already taken a significant amount of damage from a handful of battles beforehand, and he had run out of healing potions. Therefore, another fight was certainly out of the question unless he felt like dying that day. He couldn't remember which way the cave's exit was located since after a certain point every tunnel they ran through looked identical. So, he kept on running with the noblewoman hoping for luck to guide him.

Finally, they ran out into an open area of the cave where huge crystals criss-crossed each other from floor to ceiling. They lit up the area as though the moon was its light source. However, it seemed like a dead-end as Locke frantically searched for a way out until he saw that across from where they had entered, past a dense wall of crystals, was another tunnel.

"Hurry, this way!" He shouted behind him to the noblewoman as he pulled her towards the blockade of crystals. There was a medium-sized opening that the noblewoman could easily slip through and that Locke could just manage with his armor on. However, as he began to help the noblewoman over some crystals to get to the opening, the creatures that were chasing them burst out of the tunnel they had come through.

Having their prey in sight, the three Crypt Scorpions simultaneously let out a piercing shriek before they went in for the attack.

"Go, go, go!" Locke yelled to the noblewoman as he removed the spear from his back and took a defensive stance. Under most circumstances, a spear couldn't withstand against one, let alone three, Crypt Scorpions. They were the length of three adult horses and double Locke's height. Their shells were also too thick for even the most well-sharpened weapons. However, Locke's spear was different. The shaft was made of a rare metal alloy that could endure against mighty blows, yet still remain lightweight, while the spearhead was forged using nithirium - a pure metal only found in the northern regions of the Drakarias continent. It was one of Locke's prized possessions.

The noblewoman hastily ran amongst the crystals towards the opening, leaving Locke behind to defend.

One of the scorpions charged Locke head on, but he evaded the attack by rolling out of its path. Missing its target, the scorpion slammed into the crystal wall behind Locke, stunning it. The other two scorpions then came at Locke from each side. They both used their pincers to attack, but Locke dodged their blows by ducking and weaving until he saw an opening to strike one of them. During an incoming assault, Locke lunged towards the scorpion on his left and ducked under its pincer to send a firm, piercing blow right through its head with his spear. The scorpion squirmed before its limbs went limp. Locke pulled his spear from its head and jumped back against the crystals, letting the creature fall to the ground. *One down...Two to go,* Locke thought as he held his left shoulder and winced in pain. His shoulder was throbbing from a large bruise he had received earlier that day while trying to protect the noblewoman, and this battle was only putting a strain on it.

"Sir Bellorne! Are you all right?" The noblewoman shouted from the safety of the thick crystal wall.

"I'll be fine, Lady Cassia!" He shouted back. Locke watched as the other scorpion tried to attack him with its pincers again. Knowing that his back was against the crystals, Locke rolled to the side causing the scorpion's pincer to go through a gap in the crystal wall and become stuck. Locke took this chance to go in for a stab to its side but, before he could, the tail of the scorpion that had been temporarily stunned whipped him away from the crystal wall and onto the cavern floor. The force of the impact winded Locke and caused his bruised shoulder and back to ache tremendously.

"Sir Bellorne!" Lady Cassia yelled from her safety zone.

Blood dripped from the corner of Locke's mouth as he tried to force himself to stand, but he was too exhausted and in too much pain to move. *I have to get up*, he told himself as he lied on his chest. Even his vision was slightly blurred. *I really wish Zephyrous was here, but he wouldn't fit in these caves... Damn it all!*

Suddenly, a scream resonated throughout the crystal-filled area, and Locke shot his head in Lady Cassia's direction. From what he could tell, the scorpion that had thrown him was trying to claw its way through the crystals to get to her. But what could he possibly do? Locke had no more energy to spare and no unharmed part of his body to move. Then, when he thought things couldn't become worse, the scorpion that had gotten its pincer stuck ripped it from the wall in a shower of crystals and set its sight on Locke. *Damn it, damn it, damn it! I can't move!*

The furious scorpion charged at Locke with its venomous tail erect to strike but, before it got close enough to finish him off, a thin white light came crashing down on its back and sent streams of electricity throughout its body. The scorpion spasmed for a few seconds then stopped. Dead. A leg or two continued twitching, but it was definitely dead. A hooded figure then landed and kneeled down in front of Locke.

"Looks like someone's in pretty bad shape," said the figure before him. The voice was that of a female and sounded familiar. "Here, take these. We'll take care of your new friend." The figure placed two vials on the ground in front of him and ran off towards the last scorpion.

"We?" Locke questioned as he forced himself to grab each vial and chugged their contents.

With a longbow in hand, the hooded woman ran towards the last scorpion that was now busy defending against an adult, black dire wolf. The dire wolf, which was only slightly smaller than its prey, pounced onto the scorpion and sank its fangs into its side. Unfortunately, its carapace was too dense for the wolf's fangs to do much damage, but it still caused the scorpion to lash out in pain from the crushing force. The scorpion violently attempted to shake it off, but the dire wolf was too heavy and held on with the aid of its claws and jaw.

Distracted by the dire wolf on its back, the scorpion didn't notice the hooded woman taking advantage of the situation. She removed an arrow from her quiver, jumped off the crystal blockade, and propelled herself into the air above the scorpion. Then with one deadly, accurate shot from her longbow, she pierced the creature straight through its head. Unlike the other two scorpions, this one died instantly. No squirming, no spasming, nothing. The hooded woman landed with a tuck and roll, and placed her bow on her back as she stood. Her dire wolf also let its, now deceased, prey go and jumped down to where the archer stood.

After drinking the potions, Locke's wounds immediately began to heal, and he could soon see properly again. Using his spear, he lifted himself off the ground, wiped the blood from his mouth, and walked over to where the hooded woman was helping Lady Cassia out from behind the crystal wall.

"An archer with a black dire wolf..." Locke pondered aloud for a second. "Axia, is that you?"

The hooded woman looked at Locke for a moment then removed her hood to reveal a copper-skinned Elf with short, silver hair and eyes.

"Hello, Locke, it's been a while," Axia replied.

"I offer you my thanks, miss," said Lady Cassia as she bowed with the grace that only nobles excelled at.

"Yes, thank you, but how did you find us?" Locke asked as he placed his spear on his back; now strong enough not to use it as a crutch.

"I was passing through and saw Zephyrous at the cave entrance. Considering that silver dragons aren't common in this region, I figured it was you. I also figured that you'd probably lose your way in this particular cavern," Axia answered.

"I see... But how did you track me *here*, specifically?" Locke emphasised by pointing towards the ground he currently stood on.

"Simple, Shadowfang followed your scent. You and your dragon are around each other so much that you smell identical." Shadowfang then sat next to Axia and she petted under his head. "Anyway, we should go. These carcasses will attract more creatures and I doubt you want that. M'lady, I would advise that you ride on Shadowfang, it would be safer. And don't worry, he's quite harmless unless provoked."

Shadowfang lowered himself to allow Lady Cassia to mount him and, with Axia's help, she hesitantly did.

"Oh my!" Lady Cassia exclaimed in surprise as the dire wolf stood back up to its normal height. "This is very high."

"You get used to it. All right, let's get out of here."

x x x

As they exited the cave, an enormous, silver-blue dragon immediately greeted Locke.

"Hello to you too," Locke said with a chuckle and petted Zephyrous' snout. "Yes, I'm fine... Now."

"You must let me reward you in some way, miss," Lady Cassia gleefully said as she was helped down off the dire wolf by Axia.

"That isn't necessary. I just happened to be in the right place at the right time. Locke almost died trying to save you, so it's only fair that he gets whatever reward he was promised," Axia plainly explained.

Saddened by the refusal, Lady Cassia watched as Axia mounted Shadowfang.

"You're leaving already?" Locke asked in surprise. "Can you at least accompany us back to the Lady Cassia's home?"

"Sorry, but I have things to attend to. Take care." Axia nodded to the both of them before she and Shadowfang ran off into the shadows of the forest.

PART II

Hidden within the thick foliage of the forest, Axia inhaled a slow, calm breath as she drew back her bow. Her focus was sharp. Her hands were steady. Her target - a band of Human thieves around a campfire - was unaware. With a quiet exhale, she released the arrow from between her fingers and watched as it darted through the cold air of the moonlit twilight.

The arrow pierced through one of the thieves' shoulders with pin-point accuracy. He fell to the ground screaming in agony as the other three were now alerted by someone else's presence.

Without delay, Axia fired another arrow and it too hit a thief, but this time in the leg. After that shot, she quickly changed her position.

In a panic, one of the remaining thieves pulled out a crossbow and fired in the direction he had seen the second arrow come from. He then reloaded and fired again. He was obviously inexperienced because of his terrible aim and fearful gaze.

Most likely a new recruit. He'll probably faint before I can get anything out of him, Axia thought as she studied him. However, the other thief seemed relatively calm. She had drawn her weapon, an axe, but was much less frightened than her partner. *Now she's probably the band leader and might have some answers.*

"Calm down and stop wasting your shots on thin air! They probably already changed their position before you drew your crossbow," said their leader.

"But Talla..." The frantic thief tried to object, but he quickly silenced himself as Talla gave him a stern look. Although still scared, he stopped firing his bolts and waited for further instructions.

The two waited and listened for what felt like an eternity, but heard nothing. Then out of nowhere, a light whistle echoed throughout the campsite. Talla quickly reacted.

"There! They're hiding--" However, before she could finish her sentence, Shadowfang jumped out of the brush behind them and attacked the thief with the crossbow, pinning him to the ground face-first. Caught off guard, Talla tried to get her act together and attack the dire wolf with her axe, but instead she found herself suddenly falling to the ground as her feet were swept from under her. She closed her eyes from the impact to the ground and quickly felt a weight on top of her. Once Talla opened her eyes again, she was presented with two well-crafted daggers at her throat.

"I have a few questions for you," Axia calmly said.

Talla tried to reach for her axe that had fallen out of her hand, but her fingertips only grazed it.

"Think before you make a grave mistake. I only have questions and you might have answers. When I get what I need, I'll let you go."

Talla glanced over at her wounded comrades and saw that, though they were injured, it was nothing serious. Even Shadowfang only kept the frightened thief pinned down with one paw, suggesting that there was no malicious intent.

"What do you want?" Talla asked, accepting her defeat. Axia sheathed one of the blades and pulled out a rolled up paper from her back pouch.

"Have you seen him before?" Axia asked as she showed a sketch of a rogue Elven boy seemingly between fifteen and seventeen years old. Luckily, Axia didn't need to wait long for an answer.

"Ha! I couldn't forget that face if I tried! Yeah, I know this bastard!" Talla exclaimed with a loud laugh, but quickly restrained her outburst as Axia's expression darkened and her blade inched closer to her throat. "Okay, okay! He spoke with our boss once about a job to con a high ranking nobleman," Talla hastily spoke. "Everything he said was verified, so we accepted the job but, in the end, he conned *us* and fled with more than half of our loot!"

Yeah... That sounds like him, Axia thought. "What was his name? And where is he now?"

"Rel. Rel Dakar and, according to our sources, he's most likely in the City of Arris."

That's about a day's trip from here, Axia thought again in surprise.

"Our gang has been hunting him down for weeks," Talla continued.

"I see..." Axia let go of the thief.

Now free, Talla quickly picked up her axe and distanced herself from Axia. She stood and took on a defensive stance in anticipation of an attack. However, to her surprise, Axia sheathed her other dagger.

"Be sure not to pull out the arrows as they are. Break off their shafts then remove them. If you don't, you risk causing more harm." Axia explained, referring to Talla's two wounded comrades. She then motioned to Shadowfang that it was time to go and he promptly removed himself from the terrified thief. However, before they had the chance to be on their way, they felt a sudden gust of wind accompanied by an obnoxiously loud voice.

"Finally found you, Axi!"

Recognising the voice, Axia and Shadowfang immediately looked up to find Locke, with a smile on his face, and Zephyrous hovering above them.

XXX

Axia walked through the forest alongside her dire wolf while Locke followed behind them with his arms rested behind his head. Zephyrous had taken to the skies.

"How long do you intend to *accompany* me?" Axia exasperatedly asked.

"Until you explain what's going on. I don't mind the detour," Locke answered.

"I am under no obligation to explain anything to you."

"True, but you've been acting very distant. I noticed something was off ever since you, dare I say it, *rescued* me a few days ago and nothing has changed. My guess is that your problems lie with this." Locke then suddenly ran up next to Axia and pulled out the sketch of the rogue boy from her pouch. "I caught a glimpse of this in your hand when you were with that thief earlier. Who is--" Before Locke could finish his question, the paper was snatched from his hand and pinned to a neighbouring tree with a dagger.

"Don't you *ever* touch my belongings again," Axia added, speaking in an intense, yet subdued tone. She then walked up to the tree and removed the dagger along with the sketch. However, she didn't return to Shadowfang's side right away. "Listen Locke... I know you're concerned, but I rather not involve you in family matters. That's why I'm not telling you anything. So, if you wish to follow me, I won't stop you, but expect nothing else," she calmly explained without facing him.

Silence filled the air. Only the sounds of crickets, and Zephyrous' flapping wings could be heard as he hovered above until Locke finally spoke.

"I understand, but at least answer me one question: what do you mean by *family matters*?"

Axia paused then turned around and showed him the sketch. "I'm searching for my younger brother."

PART III

Dusk fell over the forest as Axia and Locke reached its edge. From that point onwards, it was flat and grassy terrain that surrounded the road that lead to the grand City of Arris.

Shadowfang jumped out from the thicker part of the forest and stood next to Axia.

"Finally..." Axia whispered to herself. She was about to proceed ahead, but Locke grabbed her shoulder and held her back.

"Wait, Shadowfang can't come with us," he said.

"What? Why not?" She demanded, surprised.

"Arris has a law which states that large animals cannot enter the city. Even its own citizens cannot have anything larger than a knee-high dog as a pet," he explained.

"And you couldn't mention this earlier?" Axia angrily questioned.

"Well, you didn't seem in the best of moods, so I thought it would be better to stay silent," Locke answered while glancing away.

Axia rolled her eyes with a groan.

Soon, Zephyrous swiftly landed next to Locke and lowered his head.

"Hello Zeph, you know the drill. I won't be gone too long, only a few days or until I call for you," he said as he petted his dragon's snout with a smile.

Axia looked up at Shadowfang who was now sitting patiently at her side. She settled her hand on his head. "Sorry boy, you'll have to stay behind this time," she sadly spoke. Shadowfang started to whimper. "Don't worry, I'll only be gone three days at the most. I'll be fine, and I'll hopefully be back with Rel." Axia stroked Shadowfang's jet black fur and hugged him. As she pulled away, he licked her cheek to which she giggled. "All right, all right. Go on and hide yourself."

Shadowfang stood up and hesitantly leapt into the thickest brush. Zephyrous gave a slow nod to Locke and took to the skies once again. The duo watched their companions leave then turned towards the road ahead of them where Arris was in view.

"By the way, why do we have a maximum of three days?" Locke inquired before they continued forward.

"Because that's how long we have to find my brother. If we don't find him within that time, then he surely left the city with a head start and my search begins again... Now, let's go."

As the duo approached the city gates, Axia was in amazement at the sheer size of the stone arch they had to pass underneath before the main entrance. It was enormous, to say the least, and was wrapped in carved writing that Axia didn't have time to stop and read. However, that wasn't all that was impressive. The main city gates, although had a much smaller archway, were shadowed by two giant, meticulously sculpted, guard statues on each side. One held a spear while the other had a shield. The wall surrounding the city was also so high that only someone very stupid or very brave would consider scaling it.

Without even noticing, Axia had stopped in awe. She had never been to this city before, only heard of it.

"Almost as impressive as the city where I met you, huh?" Locke reminisced, snapping her out of her daze.

"I take it you've been here before?" Axia asked, catching up to Locke.

"Why of course! I love these grand cities!"

"Nobles..."Axia muttered to herself with exasperation.

Once Locke and Axia reached the entrance, they were both stopped by guards.

"Excuse us, but you cannot enter with those weapons," one of the guards said.

Surprised again, Axia quickly turned to Locke and glared. Embarrassed that he had forgotten to mention Arris' law that prevented the entry of non-local weapons without a permit, Locke avoided eye contact with Axia. Instead, he just proceeded with handing over any weapons he had in his possession. Axia did the same, but made sure that Locke knew of her immense displeasure.

"Uhm... Axi, can you please stop burning a hole through my head with your glare? I'm sorry..." Locke awkwardly apologised as they walked through the city streets.

"You're lucky I can survive relatively well without my bow and daggers," Axia harshly replied before looking away and focusing on her surroundings.

The street they were on was lined with tall and elegant limestone buildings that were obviously constructed with lots of care. From what Axia could observe, it seemed that they happened to be in the commercial district of Arris, and so, there was an abundance of people shopping. However, it wasn't very hard to move around since the street itself was wide enough to accommodate the masses. In fact, most of the streets were very wide. Furthermore, the majority of people in the streets were either nobles or merchants. There were some adventurers and travelers here and there, but even their attire would have made them pass as nobles if they weren't already.

Axia looked down at her unimpressive, dark green and brown outfit and realized that she stuck out compared to the pristine and expensive clothing of everyone else. She didn't even sport any kind of jewelry except for her gold earring cuffs. Even Locke blended in with his silver and navy blue, dragonrider armor.

"You look fine. No need to worry," Locke chuckled.

"I'm not worried about how I look, but I stand out too much. If I bring too much attention to myself, and if my brother is here, he'll find out and leave as fast as he can," she said looking up at him.

"I see... That could be a problem, huh? Well, if that's the case, follow me! I know exactly where we can go to get you new clothing."

A while later, once the sun had fully set, Locke and Axia walked into a lavish inn to stay for the time they would be in the city. Axia was dressed in a leaf-green and white, short-sleeved blouse with white pants, and a brown corset. She also wore tall, brown boots; a green choker necklace, and a short, brown cloak that was black on the inside.

"I still can't believe you insisted on buying all of this... As expensive as these were I could have bought them myself," she said, dissatisfied.

Locke rolled his eyes with a light sigh.

"Let's not start this again. It was no trouble, really, but if you want you can pay for our stay here. Are those agreeable terms?" Locke asked as they approached the innkeeper's front desk.

"Welcome to our humble inn. How may I help you tonight?" The innkeeper said with a bow.

"We would like two single rooms and food for a three-day stay under Aelya Darell, please," Axia requested with an elegant demeanor and a smile.

Locke quickly glanced over at Axia, but said nothing.

The innkeeper nodded and began to prepare what was needed. He then handed them two keys, and Axia gave him a pouch of gold worth three days of accommodations.

"My thanks, Madam Darell. Your rooms will be located on the third floor. May your stay be comfortable," the innkeeper said with another bow. Axia and Locke then made their way to their designated floor.

"Aelya Darell? Let me guess, it's so that your brother doesn't know you're here, correct?" Locke asked.

Axia didn't say anything, but gave him a smirk as though silently saying that he was catching on.

Once they each arrived in front of their respective rooms, they both entered and turned in for the night.

A few hours later, Axia looked out of her window at the nearly empty cobblestone street below. Only a few drunken nobles, and city guards roamed about as she waited for an opportunity to leave undetected and really start her search for Rel. This time, Axia was wearing all black; blouse, tights, boots, gloves, and scarf. The cloak she wore was just the one from earlier, turned inside out. However, just as she was about to open the window, she heard a light knock on her door.

"Axi, it's Locke. Open up," he whispered.

Annoyed, Axia slowly opened the door. He quietly entered the room, candle in hand, and no armor.

"What do you want?" She whispered back.

"Trying to leave without me I see," he said while he observed her attire. "And when did you get those?"

"No, don't change the subject! You're not coming with me."

"Actually, yes I am. You said that I could follow you if that's what I wished, did you not?"

Unfortunately, Axia remembered saying those words back in the forest, and since she wasn't one to go back on her word she held her tongue.

Locke smirked then blew out the candle before approaching the window.

"What's your plan?" He asked.

"Once those guards are out of our sights, I'll take to the rooftops, and I guess you can take to the shadows of the streets," she explained as she walked up next to Locke. "Light clouds have rolled in tonight, which means no moonlight. This is our best chance. We'll be heading towards the center of the city."

"Why?"

"You probably never went that far in, nor noticed, but all the buildings nearest to the gate are tall and elegant. However, if you observe closely, they slowly reduce in size and beauty the farther you go towards the center. That's where we'll find the slums and possibly my brother," she said while opening the window. "You should also know that he's using an alias like me. So, look for a Rel Dakar.

Locke was impressed with Axia. He didn't expect this level of precision or thought put into every detail. Yes, he was indeed very impressed; however, this also made him more curious about why she was doing all of this. He understood that this was her brother, but to the point of changing her outfit and name... There must have been more to it. Though he didn't want to admit it, Locke really didn't know much about this female, Elven archer he called 'friend'.

Axia hopped onto the windowsill in a crouch, ready to leave. She intently watched as the guards turned a corner, then put up her hood. However, before she left, she looked back at Locke.

"Oh, and Locke?"

"Hm? What is it?"

"Don't get caught. I have enough to worry about," she bluntly stated.

Unsure if to appreciate her concern or to feel insulted, Locke remained silent.

Axia, on the other hand, didn't seem to see any problem with what she said. Taking in a deep breath, she covered her mouth with her scarf and started scaling the side of the building. Once she reached the rooftop of the inn, she jumped off onto the neighbouring rooftop and continued from there until she was lost in the darkness of the night.

From the window, Locke double-checked his surroundings for anyone who had seen what had just unfolded before closing back the window.

x x x

The slums of Arris were the complete opposite of the rest of the city. Buildings were small and made of wood or brick. Narrow, winding streets mapped out the area, but were quite busy considering the late hour, and very few guards patrolled them. In fact, the majority of the guards were stationed near the border between the slums and the main city; probably to prevent either class from entering or exiting.

Locke might have some trouble slipping past them, Axia thought as she walked the streets with open eyes and ears. She left her hood and scarf on, but no one seemed to notice or care at all. To the people who lived there, she wasn't anyone special and that was a good thing... For now, anyway. Axia knew that once she began asking around for Rel she would attract attention, which could work in her favour or against it, but certain risks had to be taken. With that in mind, she pulled out the damaged sketch of her brother from her belt and entered an inn.

By the third establishment she visited, Axia had already attracted a lot of attention. It seemed as though Rel had made quite the name for himself in the slums of Arris, and not in a good way.

"Listen, I'm not here to argue. I just need to know where he is," Axia calmly said.

"How the hell should I know? If I knew where he was he'd be dead by now!" An understandably angry merchant shouted as he slammed down a pint of ale on his table.

"Get in line, old man!" A woman shouted from further back. "We all want 'im dead!"

Rel... What have you done? Axia asked herself as the whole tavern was in an uproar.

"Listen lady, if y'ask me it's better that he ain't around. That kid's made a long list of enemies 'round these parts," the tavern bartender calmly said amongst all the ruckus.

"I see that..." She replied with disappointment, which the bartender picked up on.

"C'mere girl," he said, motioning her over. Axia approached the bar table, lowering her scarf, and he settled a pint of ale in front of her. "Now, I ain't sure why ya lookin' fer Rel, but despite his troublemakin', he was a good kid, and ya don't seem to be like those halfwits over there. So, I'll tell ya this... Rel was most likely caught by the city guards."

The tavern had coincidentally quieted enough to hear the old bartender's last sentence, and everything then fell completely silent. Axia looked around the room, and everyone's eyes were suddenly glancing away.

"These good-fer-nothin's may talk a big talk, but they'd rather believe he up and disappeared than believe he was taken by the city guards. That's how scared these fools are of 'em," the bartender explained.

"Serves 'im right if he was," a voice spoke out. The words echoed throughout the tavern and in Axia's mind.

Axia clenched her fists. "What did he do?"

"It's what he didn't do that's the easier question, girl," the bartender said.

"Stole," said the angry merchant.

"Conned," said the woman.

"Cheated," said another customer.

"Fought," said a waitress.

"S'all true, but he stayed here in the slums. Ya can get away with lots here, but for some reason Rel said he was goin' t'where all the rich are. I told 'im not to; I told 'im he was crazy. Guess he went anyway, and I ain't seen 'im since. That was about two weeks ago," the bartender continued as he took away Axia's ale, seeing that she wasn't drinking any of it.

The tavern was dead silent. No one knew what else to say, not even the old bartender. Axia contemplated the whole situation. She needed to figure out what to do next. All of her plans and ideas up until this point needed to drastically change based on this new information.

At that moment, a group of men came barging into the tavern, breaking the silence with their booming voices. With them was Locke whom they tossed into the establishment.

"Hey, this guy's looking for that kid too! He's probably with that girl!" One of the men shouted.

"Another one? And here we thought he was only popular with us!" A different drunken man shouted with a guttural laugh.

Everyone else also started laughing except for the bartender who only shook his head in disapproval.

Catching himself before falling over, Locke spotted Axia at the bar table and ran up to her.

"There you are! Did you--" Locke stopped dead in his sentence as soon as he saw Axia's face. Her head was bowed, and she was showing no sign of any emotion. He didn't know what had happened, but he knew it was nothing good.

"What happen--"

"We're leaving," she interrupted.

"But we have a while before--"

"I said we're leaving." Axia turned away from the bar table and headed towards the door. Without any other choice, Locke followed. No one stopped them or even said a word to them as they left.

XXX

A few hours before dawn, they returned to the inn without anyone suspecting that they had left. Axia removed her scarf and cloak and threw them on her bed before sitting down, head still hanging low. Instead of leaving her be and heading back to his room, Locke leaned up against a wall. He didn't feel it was a good idea to force answers out of her, so he patiently waited for them. Finally, Axia looked up at Locke.

"Rel's... In Prison."

"What?" Locke exclaimed.

"It seems that he's been here much longer than I previously thought and, apparently, he did something in the noble area to attract the attention of the city guards," she said, holding her hands.

"I'm so sorry... You came all this way to--"

"I'm getting him back."

"What?" Locke exclaimed again and quickly moved from off the wall. "Are you daft? The Arris prison is known for being very heavily guarded. If your brother is in there then it's over! He's never getting out of there!"

Axia quickly stood up and grabbed Locke by the collar of his shirt. Her stare was intense, and her words just as serious.

"Now you listen very carefully to me, Locke. There is no way in hell that I am about to let my little brother rot in prison for the rest of his life! I have two other younger siblings and a mother. Do you think I can bare the guilt of returning home, looking them in the eyes, and telling them that our brother, her son, is in prison because of foolishness? No. So, whether you like it or not, I'm getting him back and that's the end of this conversation."

The room fell so quiet that their heartbeats could almost be heard. Locke was stunned. He didn't realize how much his words would affect her.

"I'm sorry... I should have thought my words through more carefully before I said them."

Axia let him go and sat back down. She didn't once look back at him. For a long while, no one said anything. It became so awkward that Locke finally decided to head back to his room. However, before he walked out the door, he let Axia know something.

"Once we've fully rested, let me hear your plan on breaking into the prison because I'm sure you already have one."

With that, Locke left her room.

PART IV

The bright, almost blinding, light of explosions emanating from the Arris prison lit up the cloudy night sky. The thundering sounds were so distinctively loud that it awoke almost everyone in the city. Many people rushed out into the streets, or watched from the window in the safety of their homes, to bear witness to scattering debris and clouds of black smoke rising into the air.

There was no need for the guards to sound the horns because they already knew what was happening; they were under attack. By the dozen, they ran throughout the prison towards the numerous locations of the explosions. Prisoners who didn't know what was occurring could only smell the suffocating smoke and watch as shadows of feet passed in front of their cell doors. There were fires on the north, south, east, and west sections of the prison, which left the center and the basement undermanned; the perfect setting for Axia and Locke to slip right past everything. It was happening just as planned, and it couldn't have gone better.

XXX

Four days earlier, when the sun was high in the sky, Axia visited Locke's room to discuss how they would break her brother out of prison.

"What do you mean you have no plan?" Locke asked, dumbfounded, as he sat on his bed and stared at Axia who sat on a chair across from him. "Until now you've had everything figured out. What about that speech last night? About you rescuing your brother, and not feeling guilty..."

"I'm still going to accomplish that, okay?" She asserted. "I just... I just don't know how. I've never broken into a prison before." Axia stood up from her chair and started pacing back and forth.

Locke watched her then, with a mix of a groan and a sigh, he fell back on his bed. "Well, don't look at me for a solution. I want to help, I do, but the both of us don't stand a chance, and I know of no one in this city that would dare help us. Additionally, I've never broken in or out of a prison either, nor am I subtle enough for that many guards."

Axia walked over to the window and looked outside as though the answer would appear before her. *He's right. The people in the slums are too scared to go against the city, so we're still back at square one. What should I...* Axia's train of thought suddenly diverted as her eyes focused on a small spider that she hadn't noticed before crawling in the corner of the window frame. As she stared at it, her eyes widened and she apprehensively turned back to Locke. "I think I may have an idea..."

Locke's head propped up from his bed in surprise. "Really? Then what is it?"

"I know someone who can help us cause a little havoc, but we'd need to leave the city for a few days."

"Well, that's perfect!"

"Yes... But you should just be prepared for her... Uhm… Over-zealous personality."

Locke raised an eyebrow as he watched Axia scratch the back of her head out of awkwardness.

x x x

Presently inside the prison, Axia and Locke snuck through the empty corridors and made a point to keep to the shadows when random guards ran past. Axia was dressed in her all black attire from before along with her archery equipment, while Locke left behind his signature armor and only wore the brown clothing that he sported underneath it. He also brought his spear along. The only thing they had in common was a full-face, black mask to further conceal their identities.

They both stopped at a cross-section of corridors, and Axia peered down each side to check if anyone was coming. Another explosion echoed throughout the prison.

"Will she be all right? I mean, there are a lot of guards here," Locke asked, his voice muffled by the mask.

"Don't worry, she does this more often than you think," Axia nonchalantly replied.

"Didn't know you had so much faith in me, Axi," another muffled voice said from behind them.

Alarmed, the duo spun around towards the voice and found a hooded individual, dressed in a dark blue stealth outfit and wearing a similar black mask, standing before them. However, on half of this mask there was an intricately painted blue spider on it.

"N'Lea, what are you doing here? You're supposed to be keeping the guards busy!" Axia roughly whispered.

"I have, and it was fun, until I exhausted my explosives supply," N'Lea airily answered while displaying her empty satchel. "So, I thought I'd join you two, but it seems you haven't gotten very far."

Axia let out a heavy sigh and looked back down the corridors. "Just... Why don't you take care of any guards that are on their way back? Will that alleviate your boredom?"

"Yes, indeed!" N'Lea cheerfully exclaimed before running past both of her companions and down a corridor.

Locke snickered in amusement beneath his mask then continued forward behind Axia as they headed towards the basement.

XXX

Three days earlier, Axia's hands shook with fear as she clenched onto Locke while they flew through the sky on Zephyrous.

"If you were going to be so afraid, why did you suggest taking Zephyrous?" Locke asked while calmly at the reins of his dragon companion.

"Because flying is the most efficient way to get to our destination! I just didn't realise how terrifying it would be!" Axia snapped through clenched teeth, and Zephyrous let out a snort.

"She didn't mean it that way, friend, you're a brilliant flyer," Locke said to console his dragon. Axia's grip tightened and Locke spoke again. "You know, you never explained why you're searching for your brother. I have no siblings, so I can't relate to your troubles, but I'm curious."

Axia stayed quiet for a while as she thought of a way to explain the situation. "You may or may not believe me, but I come from a family of rogues."

That's easier to believe than you think, Locke thought to himself as to not interrupt her.

"I don't necessarily enjoy that lifestyle, but aside from certain other aspects, my siblings tend to revel in everything else. Both our parents taught us most of what we know. Our mother was a master thief, and our father was a master con artist. However, it was our father to whom my brother clung to the most," she continued.

"Was that bad?" Locke asked.

"Looking back... Yes. It may not mean much considering my background, but our father wasn't the most... Honourable of men and, in the end, the most important people he deceived was his own family. He just disappeared one day. It broke my brother's heart. So, when searching for him failed, Rel began travelling around trying to make a name for himself in hopes that he'd come back. It's why he only ever uses a false surname and never changes his given name."

"So, when you heard he had left home again, you decided to look for him?"

"Exactly. It had always been my mother, but as his older sister I decided to take on that responsibility this time."

The light wind, and the heavy beats of Zephyrous' wings, filled the quiet air between Axia and Locke as they both took a moment to let everything settle in their minds.

"I think I know you a little bit better now, Axi. So, thank you for that," Locke grinned. "Also, I'm glad you've calmed down now. It's nice to breathe again," he then teased to lighten the mood. Locke had wanted to get Axia's mind off her fear of flying, and his plan worked beautifully. She had completely forgotten about how high up she was, and on a dragon no less. However, Locke had not anticipated such a melancholic tale.

Not too long after, they landed in a small forest clearing. Axia, although more composed than before, still immediately jumped off Zephyrous with a new appreciation for solid ground. Locke, on the other hand, chuckled as he disembarked.

"Where do we go from here?" Locke inquired.

"This way, but Zephyrous must stay here. He'll be safer, trust me."

Locke was confused, but instructed Zephyrous to do as she said. His dragon let out a wistful huff in response.

Axia motioned to Locke to follow her out of the clearing and deeper into the forest. The trees started evenly spaced out, but the further they walked the more the trees grew denser. Soon, they had to climb over large roots, and squeeze between trees, which proved difficult for Locke because of his armor and spear that he had retrieved while leaving the city. Axia was fine, however, as though she did this all the time. In some instances, she would even jump from branch to branch to avoid certain obstacles.

She really is part rogue, Locke thought while forcing himself through some thick foliage.

"Is the almighty, Sir Bellorne, being defeated by mere trees?" Axia mocked with a smirk as she sat on a tree branch, waiting for Locke to catch up.

"I'm-- Ah!" Locke exclaimed while he stumbled back after tugging his foot loose from between some thick roots. He caught himself before he could fall and clenched his hand from the slight stinging pain on his palm. While he was struggling to free his foot, Locke had used the neighbouring tree to push against, but had scraped his hand against its rough bark in the process. "Fine... I'm just... Fine," he emphasised with a sullen look upon his face.

Axia lightly covered her mouth as she tried to suppress a grin. "You're not well-versed in forests, are you, Locke?"

"Not particularly, no."

Axia dropped down next to him with a quiet thud then placed her hands on her hips. "Well, you do seem to fly everywhere unlike Shadowfang and I, but don't worry, it's just up ahead."

"Lovely..."

"However, before we continue, let me see your hand." Axia pointed to his clenched fist. "I saw you get hurt."

"It's nothing to be concerned about," Locke tried to reassure her as he moved his hand away.

Axia rolled her eyes then forcibly grabbed his wrist.

Knowing that he didn't seem to have much choice in the matter, Locke opened his hand, though he was embarrassed to do so. The palm of his cloth glove was ripped, but the cuts on his skin weren't very deep. However, there was still a little blood and a small, dark smear.

"Hmm... You're right, it's not really something to worry about, but you should try not to touch many things with this hand until we reach our destination. I don't have anything to bandage it with, and we wouldn't want it to get infected, now would we?" Locke nodded that he understood, and Axia released his hand. "Good, then now that we've rested, let's keep moving."

Locke sighed since he dreaded the thought of walking through this forest anymore, but followed Axia nonetheless.

After a little more trekking, they finally arrived at the edge of another clearing where a medium-sized, wooden house stood in the center. It was surrounded by a large garden on the side, a shed near the back, and a wooden clothesline right beside the house.

"Why couldn't we just land here?" Locke sulked while at the same time looking exhausted.

Axia cautiously peered out through the trees. "Because they tend to attack first and ask questions later."

"Who exactly--"

Before Locke could finish his sentence, Axia noticed a small flash of light in the distance and grabbed the back of Locke's head, forcing him to duck along with her. Several throwing knives flew past their heads and firmly planted themselves into the trees behind the duo.

Caught off guard, Locke immediately gripped his spear and quickly scanned the area, but saw no one. He opened his mouth to comment on the situation but, before he could say anything, Axia dashed out into the open.

"Wait! It's me!" She shouted followed by silence. A few seconds later, an Elf emerged from one of the top windows of the house and made her way down to the ground. She was slightly shorter than Axia, but had the same copper skin and much shorter, silver hair with shaved sides.

"I know," the Elven girl plainly said, approaching Axia.

"Then why did you attack me?" Axia exclaimed.

"I didn't. I was aiming for him." The girl pointed to the bushes where Locke still remained.

"He's a friend, Annia..." Axia sighed. "Not everyone is to be attacked... Now, where's N'Lea?"

"Right here!" An over-enthusiastic voice shouted from directly behind Axia. Startled, Axia tried to react as fast as she could but, unfortunately, she was too slow. Another Elven girl, this time with long, silver hair, tackled Axia to the ground of whom let out a groan of pain and annoyance. "Always watch your back, Axi!"

Axia groaned again.

Locke, who was watching from afar in confusion, stood up to cautiously walk over to them, but found that his legs felt heavy and the sudden movement made his head spin. He held his head in his hand for a few moments until the spinning stopped then proceeded to join Axia and inquire on who the Elven girls were.

"Locke... Ow... Meet my younger sisters, Annia and N'Lea," Axia introduced, pointing to each girl while still on the ground. "The one with the long hair is who we're here for."

N'Lea stood up and grinned at Locke while he gave a forced smile in return. The dizziness then struck again.

"Locke? Are you all right?" Axia asked, her voice expressing concern.

"Just a little vertigo. I probably just need water... I have been walking around for a while in this armor and heat."

Axia lifted herself off the ground and walked up to Locke. His face was drenched in sweat beads, and his breath was quick. She placed a hand on his forehead and found that he had a high fever.

"You feel like a furnace! What happened? What did you do?"

Locke shook his head. Everything in sight was becoming a jumbled, twisted, and hazy blur. He could barely even make out Axia's face and, before he knew it, he fell to the ground.

Axia tried to catch him, but he was too heavy to hold up and they both went down. *What's wrong with him?* Axia thought in a panic. *He was fine up until now--*

"Was he injured at some point?" Annia calmly inquired, interrupting Axia's thoughts.

Axia's eyes widened as she remembered the scratches Locke had received earlier and immediately grabbed his injured hand. The cuts had turned a deep yellow with hints of green. Axia let out a quiet gasp at the infection, and Annia crouched down to examine it.

"N'Lea, help Axia get him inside, quickly," Annia instructed in a more serious tone. "He's been poisoned."

About a day later, Locke slowly awoke in an unfamiliar bed, in an equally unfamiliar room. It was small, yet cozy, and the bed was covered in soft animal fur. As he sat up, his head still felt a little groggy, but it was tremendously better than how he had felt before.

"You shouldn't get out of bed just yet," Axia said. She sat on a stool backed against the wall, near an open window, and her eyes were glued to an arrowhead she was carving.

Locke squinted from the afternoon light that poured into the room and slightly hit his face, then lied back down where he was in the shade.

"Before you ask, you've been out cold for the last day," Axia added. "The poison has only now left your system."

"Poison?" Locke tiredly asked.

"Remember when you scraped your hand on the tree? Back in the forest? Well, you accidentally crushed a special breed of small insect called a Doku. Usually, it's pretty safe and doesn't bite, but its insides are poisonous if consumed or has a point of entry into the body such as your cuts. Luckily, it's a slow reacting poison, but can still be deadly if untreated."

Locke stayed quiet for a moment before speaking again. "I guess... You've saved me again..." His voice almost sounded disappointed. Locke wasn't used to being saved since he was the one who usually did the saving. He had gone up against creatures people wouldn't wish to see in their nightmares, and men so dangerous that death was the only solution. So, the thought of being rescued twice in a row did not sit well with him, but he tried to ignore his feelings.

Axia finished carving the arrowhead and placed it in her back pouch. She then brought one of her knees up towards her chest and hugged it. "I don't deserve praise... It was my sister, Annia, who made the antidote for you. She specialises in poisons and knew the symptoms. I really didn't do much."

"Lies!" N'Lea suddenly howled while passing by the open window, startling both Axia and Locke. She carried a basket of freshly picked vegetables from their garden. "Don't be so humble! You helped carry him inside and assisted Annia with making the antidote. Although, I have to admit you didn't do much in terms of that, but you did worry about him the whole time."

Axia glared at her little sister, and N'Lea donned an innocent smile, which hid her mischievous side, then dashed away before Axia could do anything. "Shadowfang's back, by the way!"

Axia closed and locked the window, then leaned her elbow on the windowsill in annoyance. She hated when her siblings butted into conversations.

Locke suddenly started laughing, though not very strongly.

"You have quite an interesting family," he said.

"Yes... I do. I still haven't decided whether that's good or bad yet," Axia sourly replied. She looked outside and saw her sisters happily interacting with each other; N'Lea being as energetic as usual, and Annia still ever so serious. Axia then lightly smiled. "Well, I better tend to Shadowfang before he starts sulking," she insouciantly informed before standing up and walking over to the bedroom door. "We'll let you rest an extra day to regain your full strength because afterwards... We're heading back to Arris, and we're getting my brother."

Locke nodded, and Axia left the room to leave Locke in peace.

PART V

Currently, Axia and Locke ever so quietly made their way down into the prison's basement with ease, but near the bottom of the winding staircase Axia slowed down to a halt and peered down the next corridor. She reported to Locke, who had also stopped, that there were six guards stationed throughout the single corridor. Each of them already had their weapons drawn; specifically, swords and spears.

"I'll take the closest three, and you go after the others," Axia cautiously whispered. Locke nodded. Axia then exhaled a breath and snuck into the shaded part of the corridor. From there, she aimed and shot an arrow at the furthest guard of her three targets. The arrow pierced his exposed shoulder and he cried out in pain, alerting his fellow guards. Axia darted out of the shadows at the one closest to her, followed by Locke. In his moment of surprise, the guard thrust his spear at Axia, but she quickly sidestepped the attack and clubbed the guard over the head with her bow. The guard spun from the blow and fell to the stone floor, unconscious. Axia ran past him and headed for the next one.

Locke continued ahead towards his own targets. The first guard swiftly swung his sword sideways at him, but Locke blocked the attack with his spear. The metallic clang of the impact resonated throughout the corridor. Locke kept running forward, gliding his spear against his opponent's sword and, once close enough, he punched the guard in his exposed throat. The guard hoarsely coughed and staggered back. Meanwhile, another guard took the chance to rush Locke from behind with a swing from above. However, Locke swiftly stepped aside, allowing the sword to pass next to him, then took the end of his spear and struck the guard in his face. This guard immediately fell to the ground in agony as he held his profusely bleeding and broken nose. Without wasting any time, Locke swung the end of his spear to the guard's face again and knocked him out. He then turned his attention back to the first guard who was regaining some sense, and once he would be done with him he'd deal with his last target.

From inside the prison cells, the confused or scared prisoners could hear the reverberating commotion and, for some lucky few, could see the shadows of battle dancing beneath their cell doors. Every Arris prisoner was chained and bound by their ankles to the back wall of their cells regardless of the reason they were imprisoned, and Rel was no exception.

He was further down the hall, but could hear everything as clear as day. He wondered what insanity was unfolding at the prison since everything was so obnoxiously loud, but soon got his answer once the corridor commotion had ceased. A voice had called his name. A familiar voice that he wasn't expecting to hear, but he answered the call regardless.

Locke and Axia came running to the cell door from which they heard Rel's voice. Like all the others, it was a small and thick wooden door but, fortunately, they didn't need to think very hard on how to open it as they had swiped the keys from off of the now incapacitated guards. Axia removed her mask, pushed open the door and saw her brother. His curly, silver hair was in disarray; his clothes were dirty and tattered; his face was bruised. Axia was overwhelmed by frustration and solace, and she ran up to Rel to unlock the chains that had not only restrained him, but bruised him.

"Why'd you come all this way here?" Rel asked, shocked to see his sister, yet debating whether this was better than if it was his mother.

"For two reasons: because you're a hopeless fool, and because you're my brother," Axia answered and helped him to stand.

"Although it pains us to admit it sometimes," N'Lea added, unannounced, as she poked her head inside the cell and removed her mask. "By the way, I took care of the archers so it would be one less problem to worry about. You're welcome."

N'Lea? This explains far too much... Rel thought upon seeing his younger sister.

"When did you get here?" Locke exclaimed in surprise as he removed his mask as well, but N'Lea only winked in response.

Rel wanted to ask about the identity of this spear-wielding man, but his chance was prevented by N'Lea.

"Anyway, we can have a family reunion later. More guards are coming and as good as I am, I can't take all of them out myself," N'Lea warned, slipping her mask back on. "Well, I probably could, but I don't want to," she continued followed by a stretch of her arms.

Axia nodded to N'Lea then gave Rel a healing potion from her back pouch. While he downed the contents of the vial, Axia slipped on her own mask, and Locke did the same.

Once Rel's injuries were healed and everyone was in agreement, they all ran out of the basement. Their next stop was outside. However, on their way there, the path was soon blocked by a number of guards.

"Don't stop running!" N'Lea ordered as she unsheathed her rapier while running towards the small crowd of guards. She dodged an attack and, using that guard's shoulder as leverage, she jumped over him and kicked two other guards down. Then, once she landed, she quickly pivoted and stabbed the guard she had jumped over through the stomach. Axia and Locke joined in the fight to aid her.

"Rel, take this! You're not some damsel in distress!" N'Lea bluntly yelled as she kicked over a foe's fallen short sword to him. With a nod, he picked it up and joined the fight as well.

The group forced their way through the onslaught of guards, and when more arrived, they kept advancing. Axia shot at as many guards as she could while Locke watched her back and made sure none of them took her by surprise. N'Lea and Rel also worked together as a unit; they had obviously done this many times before. Rel would block; N'Lea would stab. N'Lea would parry; Rel would slash.

"This somehow reminds me of that time we were stuck in that cavern with the Dwarf and the wizard," Locke casually mentioned before he simultaneously rendered two guards unconscious with his spear.

Axia back-flipped over one guard and plunged an arrow into his side. "This really isn't the time, Locke."

"I thought it was pretty fun." Locke jabbed a guard in the face.

"If by *fun* you mean being entangled by vines from a magical bag..." Axia highlighted while she launched another arrow. "Being burned, and watched as your dire wolf was struck by a spinning morningstar attached to a rope..." She kicked the final guard in the face. "Then yes, it was indeed *fun*."

"Pessimist..." Locke frowned.

All the guards they had encountered so far had now been rendered inert, but more were on their way. Therefore, despite their exhaustion - though N'Lea found this to be very amusing - the group took the chance to sprint towards the exit before reinforcements could catch up to them. Once they were outside, everyone except for Rel stopped running until he saw that no one was following him.

"W-why did you stop?" Rel appropriately asked.

"So we can get out of here," Axia said. "Just be certain to shield your eyes once I tell you to."

She quickly removed the remaining arrow from her quiver and pointed her drawn back bow to the sky. In Elvish, she whispered a spell and, with every word, the arrowhead gradually became a brilliant white. Four white ribbons of light then descended from the arrowhead's base and spun around the arrow's shaft. It was a beautiful sight, however, it would only last a moment.

"Now--" Axia was about to yell before being promptly interrupted by an arrow piercing her through her lower back.

An archer from atop the prison, one that N'Lea had missed, had fired the shot and was about to fire another.

Axia let out a painful cry, falling towards the ground, and the charged arrow flew from her fingers in an arched trajectory. In the same instance, Locke caught her as she fell and covered both his and

Axia's eyes. N'Lea and Rel did the same despite the horror of seeing their sister impaled by an arrow.

Despite its slightly altered trajectory, the arrow still swiftly soared through the air and exploded into a magnificent star of light that lit up the sky as if it was day. A few seconds later, the light vanished and the group was able to uncover their eyes.

The guards, however, who had just arrived to bear witness to the spectacle, including the archer, were not so lucky because they had been temporarily blinded. Therefore, they could not see that, in a matter of moments, Zephyrous came diving down from the sky. They could only feel the gust of wind created by his strong wings as he landed outside the prison.

Locke quickly helped Axia off the ground and onto Zephyrous while he rushed the others to mount the great beast as well.

With everyone mounted less than comfortably, Zephyrous took to the skies with a powerful flap of his wings, leaving gouges in the earth with his talons as he pushed off the ground and flew away from the city into the darkness of the cloudy sky.

PART VI

As dawn came into full swing, Zephyrous landed in the clearing of the siblings' household. Locke hastily dismounted first, throwing his mask to the ground, and carefully proceeded to descend Axia from his dragon. He settled her on the grass and held her on her side. At the same time, Annia came running outside to see what was happening.

"What happened to Axia?" Annia demanded.

"S-She was struck by an arrow... It was my fault. I thought I had dealt with all of the archers, but I…" N'Lea paused and swallowed as though something had gotten caught in her throat. "I didn't double-check to make sure…" She explained and removed the mask that sat atop her head.

"Don't blame... Yourself. There were many guards… Even for you," Axia reassured while still in pain. "Just get me a healing potion... And I'll be right as rain," she chuckled.

Annia quickly ran back inside to see what she could find. In the meantime, Axia shifted her attention over to Rel. Mask in hand, his head hung low, and he wore a familiar expression.

"You too... Don't blame yourself. I don't regret it, but… No more foolish ventures, okay?"

Rel nodded in agreement and held back from shedding any tears. A moment later, Annia came running back with a small, purple vial.

"We have no healing potions left…" Annia informed everyone, slightly out of breath.

"Heh… Forgot I took the last one…" Axia weakly muttered.

Rel's eyes widened and he glanced away.

"But we can still use this." Annia kneeled down next to Locke and Axia, popping open the vial she had brought.

"What will that do?" Locke asked.

"It's a mixture that will cauterise the wound as well as heal. It's a better solution to using fire, which will scar you, but it'll hurt just as bad."

"Great…" Axia groaned. "All right, best get this over with… Locke, you'll need to… Remove the arrow."

Locke nervously nodded and looked around for something that she could bite down on so as to not bite her tongue. He settled his eyes on Annia's leather gloves and told her to give them to Axia. Annia did as she was told, and Axia bit down on the gloves. Locke then firmly gripped the shaft of the arrow and snapped it in half. The swift pain caused a grunt to escape Axia's lungs, but she kept herself as composed as possible, trying not to squirm too much. Locke then pulled out the other half of the arrow from Axia's torso, tossing it aside.

"Hold her down and don't let go…" Annia instructed as she held the vial over the bleeding wound.

Locke turned Axia onto her back and held her shoulders down, while Axia clenched her jaws down on the gloves more in anticipation for whatever agony she was about to endure.

Annia tilted the vial and poured the purple liquid into and around Axia's wound. Immediately upon contact with her skin, Axia jolted up from the ground with a strained scream, her teeth grinding against the leather gloves. Locke lunged forward, grabbing onto her, and forced her back on the ground. Rel and N'Lea each grabbed a leg as well to prevent her from flailing. The pain was so intense that it brought tears to Axia's eyes, as though she was being branded.

Fortunately, the pain only lasted a minute, but it was a minute Axia wouldn't soon forget. The liquid dried and hardened like snake's skin around the wound, and a cooling feeling soon set in. Locke, N'Lea, and Rel then released Axia from their grasp, seeing as she was no longer in immense pain.

Everyone stayed silent for a moment, each letting out a sigh of relief before Annia decided to speak.

"You took that better than I thought you would."

Axia groaned.

"You'll need to rest for a few days, but you'll be right as rain," Annia continued as she stood up and dusted off her knees.

"Thank the heavens," N'Lea murmured.

"Yeah…" Rel softly agreed. "By the by, thank you all for—" He managed to say before Annia hit him behind the head. "Hey!"

"You. Inside. Now."

Rel was about to protest, but upon seeing Annia's angered expression, he stood up and obediently made his way towards the house. Annia followed close behind.

Axia snickered and removed the gloves from her mouth. "My turn. If you two would be so kind…"

Locke helped Axia from off the ground, and N'Lea grabbed one of Axia's arms and swung it over her shoulders.

"Thank you," Axia tiredly said. "Also, N'Lea, let's make sure not to let mother know about all this, okay?"

"Heh, don't have to tell me twice."

The three then slowly walked towards the house.

XXX

A few days later, Locke walked out of the little wooden house and followed the sounds of clashing metal. Behind the house, he found N'Lea and Rel sparring. N'Lea held her trusty rapier while Rel used the sword he had taken from the prison, though he would only ever be able to use it for training.

Rel ran and slashed at his sister, but she deflected and pushed his sword to the side, then roundhouse kicked him in the waist.

Rel folded and held his waist.

That seems a little harsh for siblings, Locke thought with a raised eyebrow.

"Don't worry, these two do this all the time," a voice reassured him.

Startled, Locke turned to the side to find Annia standing next to him, arms folded. *When did...? How'd she...?*

"But I'll admit that N'Lea's being particularly harsh this time. It's probably because she's still mad at Rel for causing so much trouble. However, you needn't worry, Rel most likely saw this coming or he wouldn't have agreed to spar," Annia elaborated. "He already knows what I think, so I suppose this is her way of sharing her opinion."

"I... see..."

The two stood in silence as they watched Rel and N'Lea spar. For the most part, it was a fairly even fight, despite N'Lea's less-than-restrained strikes.

"Anyway, if you're looking for Axia, she's that way," Annia informed and pointed towards the forest, in the direction of the other clearing.

Locke thanked and bid her farewell before leaving and trekking through the dense forest until he emerged into the neighbouring clearing. There, Axia, sporting the expensive garments from Arris, was practicing her archery accompanied by a resting Shadowfang. Her aim was slightly off.

"Almost got it that time," Locke commented.

Axia removed an arrow from her quiver and drew back her bow with a wince. "*Almost* isn't good enough for me."

"Must you always be so serious?" He asked as she fired her arrow. It hit slightly above the center target that was painted on a tree. "Your brother is back, and you're healing up quickly. You *are* allowed to relax."

Axia was about to remove another arrow, but paused. *Maybe he's right?* She thought. *I'm becoming more like Annia.* Axia shuddered.

"Fine, you win," she said setting her archery equipment aside. She then realised that Locke was wearing his dragonrider armor. "I see you're getting ready to leave."

"Indeed! Zephyrous and I have many more places to explore, and many more damsels to impress," he boasted with a smile and a wink.

There were a few seconds of silence as Axia tried to comprehend a noble's way of thinking, or rather, Locke's way of thinking. However, this caused her to suddenly burst out laughing. A sincere and relaxed laugh Locke hadn't truly seen from her, but he also wasn't sure whether to take it as an insult or not.

"I'm sorry, not sure what just came over me," she explained while wiping a tear from her eye as she finished laughing.

Locke pouted in response, but accepted her apology. Just then, Zephyrous flew in and landed right next to Locke. It was time for them to depart.

"Well, we must be off, fair maiden. It was unexpectedly fun." Locke bowed then turned to leave.

"Wait a moment," Axia quickly said. Locke stopped and turned back. "Thank you," she smiled.

"Anytime," he smiled back. However, before he turned back towards Zephyrous, he suddenly donned a smirk. "Ahem... You know, it's customary to bestow a souvenir as gratitude for someone's aid," he said and held out his hand.

Axia folded her arms and raised an eyebrow. "Is it now?"

Locke nodded with a hint of excitement.

"I see... Well, I shan't be rude then." Axia rummaged through her pouch for a moment and removed something. Then, in Locke's hand, she promptly placed an arrowhead. "This should suffice."

"Uhm... This wasn't exactly what I had in mind..." Locke said, his voice oozing with disappointment as he stared at the little arrowhead.

"What exactly were you expecting? A necklace or handkerchief perhaps?" Axia slyly answered, and Locke glanced away. "Sorry to disappoint, but you should be honoured. I make all of my arrows from scratch, including the arrowheads. There hasn't been one that looks the same as the other from my experience. So, you possibly just received the only arrowhead of its kind, made by yours truly."

Locke looked at the arrowhead a second time then closed his hand with an impressed smile. "You are one interesting Elf."

Axia shrugged in agreement and watched as Locke mounted Zephyrous. He placed the arrowhead in one of the satchels around his dragon companion then grabbed the reins.

"May our paths cross again someday soon, Axi."

With that said, he and Zephyrous flew off into the sky as Axia and Shadowfang watched.

I'm certain they will.

FIN

A WORD FROM THE AUTHOR

I hope you enjoyed reading the second edition of *Crossroads*! If you're someone who previously read the first version of this story then you might notice a few differences. If not, then welcome aboard!

I had been meaning to polish up this story for a while, but I always figured that the old version was okay because it acted as a sort of time-capsule. However, you can only leave something for so long before you just can't help but try to fix it. So, that's what I did! Not only that, but I added illustrations too (such talented artists)!

Anyway, thanks for reading! <3

Sincerely,

CROSSROADS: Scales of Fate

PART I

The warm rays of the sun beamed down on the small port town of Pailaal and reflected off the golden-coloured rooftops for which the town was known for. Its buildings were short, wide, and built so sturdy that a typhoon could only leave scratches, and its citizens could also be described as such.

The streets were hustling and bustling; packed to the brim with all sorts of characters from lowlifes to disguised nobles, and merchants shouting from every angle at anyone who passed by their stalls. Everything from food morsels to animal droppings also lined the streets, making it a walking hazard for anyone dumb enough to wear their best footwear.

However, despite its outer appearance, Pailaal was quite a wealthy town because it imported various foreign and rare items. This in turn attracted many rich individuals, and N'Lea had her eyes on each and every one of them.

"Don't even think about it," Annia quietly said as she examined a vial of grinded, brown powder at a merchant's stall.

"Hey, it's not my fault he thought placing his money there was a good idea," N'Lea responded while she casually eyed a man across the street who had a small bag tightly tied around his belt. "I bet you ten silver coins I can get there and back without him even realising he's broke until tonight."

Annia set the vial down on the stall's table, gave a nod to the disappointed merchant, and looked at her twin sister. "Why would I agree to a losing bet?" Annia asked in her signature stoic voice before walking into the stream of people headed further into town.

N'Lea let out a dejected groan then pushed her way through the crowd to follow Annia.

"Come on! This guy's really asking for it. If I don't steal it, someone else will."

"Then I want half of anything you take," Annia said.

N'Lea quickly silenced herself. She had no intention of sharing anything she stole and because she knew Annia well, even if she stole anything behind her back, Annia would find out and wouldn't rest until she got her share. So, through a huff and a pout, N'Lea dropped the subject.

After quietly following the flow of people for a while, the Elven sisters both walked out of the crowd and into the town square. It was a fairly large area and the only place in town that had some semblance of decency as there was far less traffic, which meant far less trash. It was also illegal for merchants to set up their stalls in the area. The one and only thing in the square that remained pristine, as though it had just been carved, was a limestone fountain in the shape of a serpent. But not just any serpent… A Leviathan. The basin of the fountain was the Leviathan's winding body, then its spiked head rose up high to look towards the sea. It was from its fanged, opened mouth that the fountain's water continuously cascaded.

Annia walked up to the fountain and sat down on its edge. She removed a leather-bound journal from her travel bag and crossed out several things on a list. N'Lea, on the other hand, remained standing with a perpetual scowl across her face as she tried to suppress her urge to steal from all the naïve passing folk.

"Did we get everything?" She asked, trying to divert her thoughts to something else.

Annia glanced up from her journal at N'Lea and raised an eyebrow. "*I* got everything we were supposed to."

"Yeah yeah," N'Lea said as she accentuated each word with a dismissive wave of her hand. "Was there anything else *we* were supposed to do?"

"No. We're free to do whatever we want now." Annia closed her journal and placed it back in her bag.

"Perfect! Then I propose we get something to eat!" N'Lea's eyes gleamed. "I may not be able to fill my pockets, but I'll be damned if I don't fill my stomach! I overheard some Dwarves talking about this tavern nearby that has the best dumplings, so let's go!" N'Lea grabbed her sister by the wrists and pulled her to her feet.

"I guess we could do that. We have enough money left over," Annia agreed, her serious tone softened by the thought of Pailaanese food.

N'Lea grinned from ear to ear and, with a spring in her step, she pulled Annia in the direction of the tavern she had heard about.

XXX

It took longer than expected, but the girls eventually found the tavern hidden away at the end of a side street. A good location if one wanted to avoid most of the traffic of the main streets.

It wasn't a very big tavern and the windows were small, but the burgundy-coloured window frames and matching curtain-covered doorway gave it a welcoming feeling. There was also a wooden sign that read 'The Coalstone,' which hung from a pole that extended out from the establishment. Part of the street was also wet due to a toppled over barrel of water from a shop across the street.

"Here we are! It looks a lot more presentable than I expected," N'Lea mentioned.

Suddenly, their attention shifted towards the doorway as a crash, like something had been thrown, emanated from inside the tavern. The girls glanced at each other in confusion then back at the doorway. A few more crashes and thuds soon followed.

"Guess we're just in time for a fight," Annia casually commented. "Maybe the inside might fit what you had imagined."

"Oh! I want to see this!" N'Lea exclaimed in excitement.

Annia didn't protest but watched as N'Lea approached the curtain and moved it aside to see what mischief was happening inside The Coalstone. However, as soon as she did, a man wearing royal-blue garments, and clenching a broomstick, was hurled in her exact direction.

Annia, having very little time to react, grabbed N'Lea by the collar of her blouse and pulled her out of the way.

The man in question flew past the girls and crashed onto the wet cobblestone street with an added roll that turned his back towards the tavern.

"Whoa! Thanks for—" N'Lea was about to say to Annia until a loud, deep, and angry voice caught her attention.

"Get up, you shameless wazzock!" A Half-Orc, wearing fisherman's gear, yelled with a growl in his voice as he stepped out of the tavern. He dragged two wooden chairs behind him. "We're not done! Not until I break both your knees!"

The man on the ground coughed a few times then gradually lifted himself up until he was in a sitting position - one knee pulled up and facing the tavern. He rubbed his head from the slight throbbing pain. "Ow… Isn't that a little excessive?"

Upon seeing the man's face, Annia's and N'lea's eyes widened with surprise. "Locke?"

"Huh?" Locke wondered then looked over at the girls. "Wait… Annia? N'Lea? What are you two doing here?"

"That's what we would like to know," N'Lea answered before the fisherman cut the conversation short by rushing towards Locke and bringing one of the chairs down where he sat.

Locke dove to the side, broomstick still in hand, and the chair hit the cobblestones with such force that the legs broke and scattered about the street.

Locke stood up and addressed the Elven twins. "Sorry you two, but let's chat after I've dealt with this mongrel."

The fisherman tossed aside what remained of the wrecked chair. "Deal with me? With that?" He mocked as he pointed to the broomstick in Locke's hand.

"Well, considering you have a chair, I think this is quite appropriate." Locke smiled then widened his stance and pointed the end of the broom handle towards the fisherman.

Angered by Locke's unwavering arrogance, the fisherman raised the second chair in the air and ran towards him. Locke also dashed towards the fisherman who, once close enough, repeated his last attack. Locke, however, dropped to the ground and slid underneath him, allowing the second chair to become just as destroyed as its predecessor upon contact with the wet street. From behind the fisherman, Locke quickly took the broomstick and jabbed behind his right knee to bring him closer to the ground. He then jumped onto the fisherman's back and secured his position by tightly wrapping his legs around his torso and placing the broomstick around his throat.

"Should we be doing something to help?" N'Lea asked, arms folded, as she watched the fisherman attempt to violently shake Locke off.

"Don't get involved in things that don't concern you," Annia answered despite her eyes thinning as she intently watched the fight as well.

Gasping for air, the fisherman backed up against a neighbouring building's wall and repeatedly hit against it until Locke loosened his grip. He then grabbed Locke's arm and threw him over his shoulder and onto the cobblestones once again.

Locke let out a loud grunt from the impact. *I wish I had my armor...* He thought through the throbbing pain that lined his back.

"Not so smug now, are you?" The fisherman yelled as he was about to pierce Locke through the stomach with the splintered and jagged wooden edge of what was left of the second chair. However, before that could happen, he felt two small pricks on the side of his neck, like mosquito bites. The fisherman touched his neck where he had felt the pricks and discovered two needle-sized darts.

"I suggest you move unless you want the brute to fall on you," Annia said aloud to Locke as she tucked away a very thin blow-dart.

“I thought you said not to interfere…” N’Lea whispered to Annia, but did not get an answer in return.

After hearing Annia’s advice, Locke tilted back his head and saw that the fisherman was wobbling from side to side. And so, in a bit of a panic, Locke hastily sat up and moved out of the way before the Half-Orc fisherman fell to the ground, unconscious.

“By the heavens, what did you do to him?” Locke asked.

“I just gave him a small dose of Nightbane. He’ll be asleep for a while,” Annia replied as she and N’Lea approached. “Anyway, unless you want more of an audience than what you’ve already acquired then I also suggest we leave.”

Locke hadn’t noticed, but his fight had attracted more than just the patrons from The Coalstone. Some people from off the main streets, some living in the nearby buildings, and nearby shop owners had all seen the fight and were whispering different things to each other. The owner of the tavern also stood near the entrance, peering past the burgundy curtain.

“Oh… Yes… You may have a point,” Locke agreed with an embarrassed smile. He then stood up and wiped what he could off of his partly damp outfit. “But first, let me deal with something.” Locke walked over to the tavern owner and removed from inside of his garment a pouch of gold coins. He placed it in the owner’s hand and apologized for the mess before rejoining the girls.

“Finally… We can get something to eat!” Annia exclaimed.

The three of them then calmly walked away as the crowd of onlookers tried to attend to the fallen fisherman.

XXX

Seated around a table at another tavern across town, the girls filled their bellies with meat buns, dumplings, seafood, and whatever else their appetites desired; a treat as thanks from Locke. N’Lea practically devoured what was in front of her, while Annia took her time. Locke, however, had already eaten beforehand and only indulged himself with a fine red wine.

"So… What did you do to make that Half-Orc so angry with you?" Annia asked.

Locke nearly choked on his drink. "Uhm… I may have unknowingly flirted with his wife…"

The girls both glanced at each other then looked back at him. They were not impressed. "You really are shameless…" They said in unison.

"I- I swear, I didn't know! Besides, she was the one who approached me…"

"Maybe I shouldn't have intervened," Annia said under her breath as she took a bite out of a meat bun.

Locke sighed and took a swig of his wine.

"Anyway, tell me, why are you girls in a place like Pailaal?" He asked, changing the subject.

"We had errands to run with our mother," N'Lea mumbled with her mouth full of food. "And before you ask, no, it's just us. Rel has been bound to the house for the past year, and Axia left for some reason or another."

"Oh? Where did she go?" Locke inquired, a bit more interested and less flustered.

"No one knows, she just up and left in a hurry. Not uncommon in our household."

"She's headed towards the Tersian border," Annia calmly interjected. "She received a letter from someone the day before she left."

Of course she found out… N'Lea thought with a hint of irritation.

"Oh really…" Locke managed to say before trailing off. He leaned back on his chair and stroked his chin in thought.

Annia and N'Lea stared at him for a moment as a grin formed on his face.

"Do you know how far along she is on her journey?" Locke soon asked.

N'Lea tossed the last dumpling in her mouth. "Well…" She started before pausing to swallow. "She left five days ago… And if she's headed towards Tersia, like Annia said, then she's probably almost there."

"In that case, I should leave if I want to catch up to her." Locke placed several silver coins on the table and stood up. "It was nice seeing you two again. Give Rel my regards, will you?"

He nodded goodbye to the girls but, before he could leave the table, Annia stopped him.

"Before you go, can you do us a small favour?" She asked.

Locke was apprehensive to answer. Not because he was opposed to helping them, not at all, but because they didn't seem the type to ask for favours. Even when Locke had helped Axia in finding her brother, she never once explicitly asked for his help. She had only accepted the fact that no matter what she said he would have stuck around. Thus, Annia's request had thrown him off, but he agreed nonetheless.

"Uhm… All right, what is it?"

To be continued in 'CROSSROADS: Scales of Fate' (Book 2)…

www.ingramcontent.com/pod-product-compliance
Lightning Source LLC
Chambersburg PA
CBHW021619030826
48979CB00033B/180
9780995048720